To Eve

PHILOMEL BOOKS
A division of Penguin Young Readers Group.
Published by The Penguin Group.
Penguin Group (USA) Inc., 375 Hudson Street, New York, NY 10014, U.S.A.
Penguin Group (Canada), 90 Eglinton Avenue East, Suite 700, Toronto, Ontario M4P 2Y3, Canada
(a division of Pearson Penguin Canada Inc.).
Penguin Books Ltd, 80 Strand, London WC2R 0RL, England.
Penguin Ireland, 25 St. Stephen's Green, Dublin 2, Ireland (a division of Penguin Books Ltd).
Penguin Group (Australia), 250 Camberwell Road, Camberwell, Victoria 3124, Australia
(a division of Pearson Australia Group Pty Ltd).
Penguin Books India Pvt Ltd, 11 Community Centre, Panchsheel Park, New Delhi—110 017, India.
Penguin Group (NZ), 67 Apollo Drive, Rosedale, North Shore 0632, New Zealand
(a division of Pearson New Zealand Ltd.).
Penguin Books (South Africa) (Pty) Ltd, 24 Sturdee Avenue, Rosebank, Johannesburg 2196, South Africa.
Penguin Books Ltd, Registered Offices: 80 Strand, London WC2R 0RL, England.

Published in Great Britain by Gullane Children's Books.

Manufactured in Malaysia by Imago

Library of Congress Cataloging-in-Publication Data is available upon request.

ISBN 978-0-399-25247-1

1 3 5 7 9 10 8 6 4 2

Something to Do

David Lucas

PHILOMEL BOOKS ✩ PENGUIN YOUNG READERS GROUP

There's nothing to do.

There's nothing to do.

Wake up, sleepy bear.

There's nothing to do.

We'll go for a walk . . .

. . . a long walk.

Still nothing.

A stick!
Now we've got something to do.

Snap.

Look! A line.

Look! Another line.

Look! A ladder.

Good-bye, ladder!

Look! Stars.

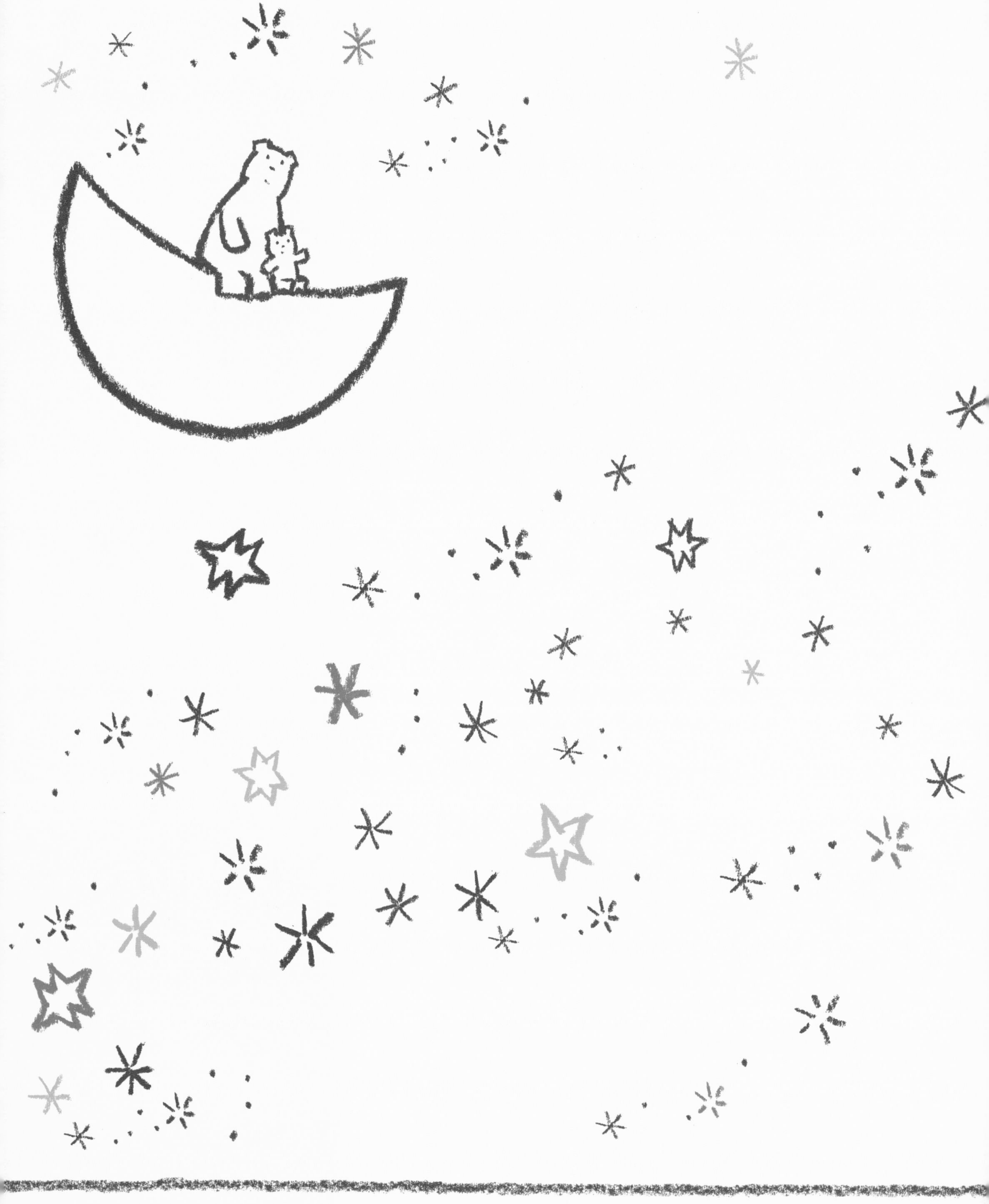

Look! A shooting star.

I'm tired.
I'm hungry.

Look! A house.

Knock knock!

Did you find something to do?

A little something!